A Romanian native, Catalin Matyus has been a resident of Long Island, NY, since 2005.

Prior to settling in the United States, Catalin traveled to nearly every corner of the world working for Princess Cruises.

In 2008, he married Tricia, and together they have two children.

The interest for writing came together with the birth of his oldest son, and the wonder and joy in a child's eyes every time they hear a story about one of their magic heroes were the driving influence in starting and finishing the book before you.

Catalin believes that all of us have found ourselves, many times growing up, in the same situations as the great Easter Bunny, where we needed an extra dose of courage to overcome certain obstacles.

He hopes that everyone will enjoy this story while being inspired by the spirit of courage and goodwill our spring hero displayed from a young age.

The First Interview with the Easter Bunny

with

Catalin Matyus

AUSTIN MACAULEY PUBLISHERS™

LONDON • CAMBRIDGE • NEW YORK • SHARJAH

Copyright © Catalin Matyus (2020)

Ordering Information:
Quantity sales: special discounts are available on quantity purchases by corporations, associations, and others. For details, contact the publisher at the address below.

Publisher's Cataloging-in-Publication data
Matyus, Catalin
The First Interview with the Easter Bunny

ISBN 9781645751304 (Paperback)
ISBN 9781645751298 (Hardback)
ISBN 9781645751311 (ePub e-book)

Library of Congress Control Number: 2020904917

www.austinmacauley.com/us

First Published (2020)
Austin Macauley Publishers LLC
40 Wall Street, 28th Floor
New York, NY 10005
USA
mail-usa@austinmacauley.com
+1 (646) 5125767

I dedicate this story to you, the reader, for every book holds the secret to an undiscovered universe.

Once, long ago, in a hidden treehouse,
A little bunny was born, the size of a mouse.
He was so tiny, so puny and thin, all other animals just
made fun of him.
Always so meek and ready to run out in the woods did not
have much fun.

Just one friend he knew, who would not make him shiver;
it was his buddy, the beaver who lived by the river.
They were always together and had lots of fun, but never
before their chores were all done.
In school were good also and never too loud; they made
their parents, all be very proud!
But our bunny grew in one year like others in ten, those
carrots and veggies had done him so well.
Yes, my friends, he grew, and he grew rather fast; first
were the ears, his bunny tail last...
He was no longer scared or ready to run; he was now a
young fellow loved by everyone.
Well, anyway, let's go ahead and begin our story, and
see what brought our bunny such well-deserved glory.

"Mister B, if you please, sir, with your voice that sounds so funny, tell us how you became the most famous bunny."

"Thank you, Mister Beaver, thank you very much, your wonderful introduction has me very touched... And yes, I would love to share with you the story, that brought me long ago such humbling glory.

It all happened a few hundred years back, I was a young bunny working in Santa's workshop.

Christmas was long gone by now and the spring was just near, as one day, I was taking my morning walk through the woods, admiring life reappear.

And as I was walking like that, breathing in the fresh air, I noticed a little egg on the ground, that didn't belong there...

'Poor little thing,' I said, 'must've fell off I guess, looking up in the trees for its cushiony nest.'

I looked and I looked, all over the trees, but all I could
see was a nest full of bees.
'Pardon me, Your Majesty,' as I bow to the queen, 'a
little egg I found, its nest have you seen?
'I have,' said the queen with a royalty frown, 'it is a
killdeer's egg, they nest on the ground.
'My guards chased away an old weasel called Ghilly,
the old thief for days, has been planning
to steal it.
'Don't worry,' she said, 'he will never be back, my army
of bees made sure of all that.'

'Thank you, Your Grace,' I said again with a bow, 'I will look through these bushes for a nest on the ground.'
So I looked all around, I walked up, I walked down, and not before long I found it...it was perfectly round.
But just as I put back the egg in that cushiony nest, the sky became darker, the wind started blowing, and the lightnings and thunders made us all really worried...
For it was him!!!
The grumpy, gray cloud, who was always so loud—as loud as a train—and if you stayed in his path, you'd get soaked with cold rain.
Even the great pines of the north with their heads like a spear, would curl in great fear every time he'd appear.
Those thunders and lightnings gave us all so much fright, so I hid inside a tree trunk, it was kinda tight.
The rain came down heavy, the wind blowing loud, and we all really hoped the sun would come out.
He did at one point for a minute or two, but the gray cloud was thick, he couldn't pierce through.
They fought like that for ten days my friend, and no one had hopes it would come to an end.
No one, but one little creature from a tight, little tree trunk, who to be honest had had quite enough...
Yes, you guessed it!
It was I, the mighty rabbit, and what I'm about to tell you was not in my habit...

I came out my tree trunk, took air in my chest, and let out a
big shout that stopped both in their quest.
'STOOOP!!!'
I yelled...and they stopped. 'For what all this fight, when
you are both needed, your rain and your light;
'You give us water to feed all the plants and you give us
warm light to grow all that stands!'
The two looked at each other and they couldn't believe, that
a creature like me would stand in between...
'You know?' said the sun... 'He is kind of right, we are
both needed, your water, my light.'
'Yes,' the gray cloud replied back, 'the rabbit is right, we
are both needed, my water, your light...
'We are both helpers of Mother Nature, she creates life
we help her nurture.'

And just as they hugged with a promise for peace, the
most beautiful thing had risen from the hills.
A river of colors, like millions of flowers; we all stared at
it for at least two, three hours.
It was the rainbow, that magical sight, it gives you much
courage, you'll lose all your fright.
But when Santa caught news of such a brave act, he
called for all creatures to his north Christmas shop.
A cloud of mystery was floating around, and all creatures
wondered what would old Kringle want...
So from all the far corners, the big and the small, we all
rushed together up to North Pole.

The castle gates opened
The waiting was done
It's a good thing that happened
My patience was gone...
And yes!
It is Santa that shows from behind
He waves and he smiles
He winks with one eye...
'Hello ho, ho, ho!!!'
'Hello,' we said back...
'Who is this creature that brought the spring back, with
such bravery act?
From the crowd I appear, walking shy towards him,
though the crowd making way made me feel like a king!
The old man looks at me and he looks kind of stunned, for
he couldn't believe that I was the brave one.
'A shy little bunny? asked the old man, amazed.
'A shy little bunny put the two in their place?
'Hmm...'
'Now that is something that we all should admire, a brave
little rabbit putting out such big fire.'
'Well,' says old Kringle, as he turns to the crowd.
'This kind of news always makes me feel proud.
'In life, there'll be things, that will turn your fur spear, but
if you show little courage, you will lose all your fear.

'So let this be a lesson for all, big and small, a gray day
can sometimes end up with a rainbow.
'And therefore, my friends from far and from near, the
bunny will be the first one to greet spring each year. And
for being so brave and not fear at all, you'll also become the
guardian of the rainbow!'
The crowd started cheering, they were shouting Ahoy and
the birds in the sky were all flying with joy!
Just one little gray bird that needed some rest, sat on top
of the rainbow and decided to nest...

A week she sat there, could've been maybe two, when a
chick's head popped out, his color was blue.
Everyone whispered softly, 'This cannot be true...'
'A gray bird like that have a chick that's all blue?
Only'n old owl with a big top hat, only he seemed to know
the answer to that...
'Of course it's the rainbow,'
said the old bird with a head like a ghoul.
'How else would a gray bird have a chick
that looks blue?
All the birds realized that the owl was wise, and moved
all their eggs on the rainbow to nest.
Some chicks came out orange, some others came blue,
some came out in yellow and I've seen purple too. They
were all flying up high on a clear blue sky, giving us such a
sight, a spectator's delight.

But the place got quite crowded, got crowded quite fast,
'cause now all the birds wanted on the rainbow to nest. A
solution was needed... There was no time to rest, how to
help all the birds on the rainbow to nest?
I thought and I thought for a day maybe two, and then
just like that an idea came through. An idea so wise and
the best part of it!!! It was in front of my eyes!
'Well, my dear friends, if you recall, Santa has just
made me the guardian of the rainbow.
'And since that river of colors was now in my keep, why
not have the birds bring me their eggs for a coloring dip?
And that's how my friends, since then, every year, I'm
coloring eggs as Easter comes near. So if you behave
and stay good the whole year, I'll bring you some color
from my river of cheer... And since Santa at Christmas
has too many to drop, I'll too bring you a present that will
make your heart hop."

The End

CPSIA information can be obtained
at www.ICGtesting.com
Printed in the USA
BVHW020219310820
587666BV00019B/120

9 781645 751298